YOU ARE UNIQUE

EXCITING AND WONDERFUL STORIES FOR KIDS ABOUT SELF-AWARENESS, COURAGE AND GRATITUDE

ANNABELLE LINDGREEN

ISBN – 9798717333313

TABLE OF CONTENTS

Introduction 1

Story 1 – The Girl Who Climbed 2

Story 2 – Ultimate Rider 7

Story 3 – Royal Beauty.. 11

Story 4 – The Free Gift 16

Story 5 – Truth Be Told 21

Story 6 – The Lemonade Stand 26

Story 7 – The Drum Teacher.. 30

Story 8 – The Summer Party 35

Disclaimer 39

INTRODUCTION

I have always thought that one of the best things about being a child is the refreshing and exciting experience of discovering new things. With every new day, there is a chance to learn something inspiring and different from seemingly simple experiences that adults have stopped to consider or value over the years.

But what if these new discoveries aren't just about other people and their situations? What if these situations are about you and the wonderfully unique life that you live? No two people can be the same, so why try to be like others when you can be the best version of yourself? The things that make us stand out are sometimes not appreciated or praised, but they will always be what builds our characters.

In this book, I hope to share stories with you which do just that. Stories which show that you are special in every single way, not just to your parents or siblings or friends, but you are special to you. Cherish every aspect of yourself, and remember that what makes you unique is as beautiful as can be.

Now, settle down and enjoy these beautifully illustrated stories as you enter into the mini worlds of our courageous characters. Maybe, someday soon, you'll also have your own special stories to share.

STORY 1 – THE GIRL WHO CLIMBED

It didn't take long for Tomi to reach the top of the old pear tree in her back garden. Branch by branch, each step was carefully placed as she reached up and pulled herself higher and higher until she got to her special seating place. She smiled as she settled down, looking out across her neighbourhood, or as she preferred to call it, Tomi's Kingdom.

"Two minutes," she said out loud, checking the time on the sky blue wristwatch Mummy and Daddy had given her on her ninth birthday last month. "I can do better next time."

She had always been a fast climber, even though her annoying older brother, Ayo, insisted he was a better athlete because he beat her every time they raced to the school gates. He only won because he always flapped his hands wildly as he ran down the narrow pavement. He flapped so hard, she had to stay a few steps back to avoid being hit by his gangly limbs.

It could also have been because he had ridiculously long legs which helped him leap much further than she could with her own stubby legs. It really wasn't fair since he was older than her and always growing taller before she could catch up.

But Tomi never got upset about her short legs because that didn't matter for what she loved doing best. Ayo could run as fast as the wind, but when it came to climbing trees, she always came up trumps. It didn't matter how high the tree was, if the branches were low enough to grab, she was sure to conquer any height.

"Girls shouldn't climb trees," Ayo said with a scowl when she had first reached the top.

"Why not?" she asked with a deeper frown, looking down on him from her great height.

"Everyone knows climbing is for boys," Ayo growled and shook his head.

"But I've got legs and you've got legs, so where's the sense in that?" Tomi had asked.

Ayo looked unsure. "Well, if you fall and hurt yourself, you'll cry like a girl."

"But boys cry just the same as girls," was Tomi's reply as she crossed her arms. "You cried when you hurt your knee at the park."

At this, Ayo got quite upset and hopped back down. He stamped his feet in protest and set off to find Daddy. Tomi sat still in fear, not sure what Daddy would say when he came out and saw her all the way up high.

But Daddy had laughed and said it was fine.

"Girls can climb just as well as boys," he said with a smile. "Maybe, one day, you'll learn to climb so well, you'll make it to the Olympics and even Ayo will cheer. But first, let's make sure you don't hurt yourself before then."

So Daddy placed large cushions at the bottom of the tree to make sure it was safe for Tomi to climb every day and grow stronger. Even when the kids at school thought it was odd, she knew it was not, because Daddy said so.

On that hot Thursday evening, school was out and Tomi's homework was all done. She propped herself up against the branch to inspect her kingdom. When she was that high up, she always felt like the queen of her pear tree castle.

"Be careful up there, Little Climber," Mummy called from the house. She knew it was safe, but she could never be certain.

"I have to make sure my kingdom is okay," Tomi called back, but she held on tighter, just in case.

Raising her hand to shield her eyes, she looked out over her kingdom and smiled at all the familiar sights from her special spot.

There was Mr. Johnson mowing his lawn as he sighed in the heat, and a little way off was Mrs. Boateng greeting the grocery van driver as he dropped off her weekly shopping. To the north, a frail looking man, all grey and wrinkled, watered potted plants on the deck in his back garden as his dog barked at a squirrel up a large apple tree.

She could even see Ayo playing football with his friends in the field at the end of the road. He was really good at kicking a ball, but she had her trees and didn't need much else at all.

Tomi sighed with content. Everything looked in order in her small kingdom on Bower Street. It was time to climb down for some much needed lemonade. The sun was so hot and she was sweating a lot. She was just about to step down when a pretty blue bird flew past, right over her head.

Tomi's head turned to follow the bird, but what she saw right then made her stop and gasp in pure shock. For at that very moment, the wrinkly old man's dog took a leap at the squirrel and hit its small head on the large apple tree. The poor old man rushed forward, not seeing a puddle. His foot hit the water and he slipped with a cry, then fell flat on his back on the deck in his garden.

"Oh no!" Tomi cried out. "Get up, mister."

But the old man didn't get up. Perhaps he couldn't hear her from so far away.

"Get up, mister," she yelled even louder, hoping her small voice would carry that far.

His dog barked and barked, but the man didn't rise.

Thinking hard for a moment, Tomi knew she had to help. She scaled down the pear tree as quickly as her stubby legs could carry her down the branches.

"Mummy, Mummy, Mummy!"

She was out of breath as she ran into the house. Mummy was in the study with her glasses perched on the end of her nose. She was typing on her laptop, her work was important, but Ayo knew this couldn't wait.

"What's wrong, Little Climber? You're quite out of breath."

"There's an old man in a garden. He fell and can't get up."

Without waiting a second, Mummy jumped up to help. "What man? What house? We'll have to go fast."

Tomi thought for a moment, but came up with nothing. There weren't any house numbers on back garden doors. "There is a great big apple tree and a deck around the back."

Mummy shook her head because that wasn't enough. But she also knew another way to help find the man.

"You'll have to go back up and tell me what else you see. But please be careful, Little Climber, we don't want you falling."

Tomi nodded quickly and climbed as carefully as she could. When she was high up once more, she looked out again. The dog was still barking and the old man still hadn't moved.

"I see a blue slate roof and a red chimney with a big round chimneypot right at the top. And, at the front, there's a tall black street lamp beside a green bus stop."

"That must be number nine," Mummy declared as she punched the emergency services number into her phone, "old Mr. Potter lives alone in there."

As Mummy called for an ambulance, Tomi stayed on the tree to keep watch over Mr. Potter and his dog. Not long after, they heard the loud wailing sound of a siren approaching Bower Street.

"They are here! They are here!" she cried and Mummy sighed with great relief.

When Ayo and Daddy came home later on, Mummy told them all about how Tomi had saved Mr. Potter's life by acting with speed.

"And all because she was up that pear tree."

Tomi was shocked when Ayo came over and gave her a hug.

"I'm sorry I said that girls shouldn't climb," he said with a big proud smile. "Because of you, Mr. Potter was saved. Don't ever let anyone say you can't do something just because you're a girl. You never know what skills could come in handy at any point in life."

STORY 2 — ULTIMATE RIDER

Joe had never seen a horse before.

Actually, that wasn't completely true. He had read all about them in books, and had seen them on telly as they trotted in shows. He had even seen a few in the distance as he looked through the window of a fast moving train. He had just never seen one up close like that day.

The thing that stunned him the most was how magnificent and tall the chestnut horse was as it sniffed at his hair with its long velvety muzzle. To be fair, almost everyone and everything stood taller than Joe. That's just the way life was for kids like him in wheelchairs.

"She's called Ember. She's a gentle creature and a great racer," Farmer Al said with pride as he brushed down the horse's mane. "Would you like to ride?"

Joe and his dad had come to the countryside to visit Uncle Albert, Aunty May and his cousin, Bobby, for a week. They didn't live on a farm, but right next to one. When Joe said he'd never been on a farm, Farmer Al had been happy to have them all come over for a while.

They'd been to the cowshed and seen all the cows. Black and white patched ones, and a bull with pointy horns. They'd been to the coop and seen all the chickens. These clucked and laid eggs on a bed of wood shavings. They'd been to the pigsty and seen all the pigs. Pink and potbellied, they weren't that filthy at all.

And now, Joe had finally met the amazing animal he'd dreamt of all along.

For years, he'd stayed up late at night in his room, looking at the horses on the pages of his favourite books. With brown, white and black silky coats, all glossy and regal as they ran in fields of green grass or bright yellow flowers. He'd watched all the equestrian shows with smart riders in black hats as they raced down long windy tracks or jumped many high hurdles.

Every single time, Joe had closed his eyes and pictured himself up on the back of those horses. Lost in his mind's eye, he could almost feel the rushing wind blowing in his face as his horse galloped fast through the wet morning grass. He could almost feel his heart pounding quickly in his chest as he held the reins tightly and left all his worries behind.

But best of all, Joe loved to capture his dreams in sketches. With his pencils and ink, he drew himself riding on beautiful horses. In fields, on tracks, and even out in a sandy desert.

So, that day, as he heard Farmer Al ask his cousin if he wanted to ride the chestnut coloured horse, Joe held back his tears as Bobby got on her back. He watched as they trotted and cantered and galloped, and he did his best to smile through it all. But right at the end, he couldn't bear it anymore.

"What's wrong?" Farmer Al asked, when he saw Joe's face fall.

"It's such a shame, I'll never know what it's like to be up there like him."

Joe's dad came up behind him and patted his shoulder. It made Joe feel a little better, but not all the way through.

"You never know what could happen if you hold on to your dreams," Dad said. "Keep dreaming big, Joe. It costs nothing at all."

That night, Joe sat up and drew all he had seen that day. The cows with the bull, the chickens in their coop, and the potbellied pigs. And last of all, he sketched a great, big chestnut horse, with a little boy riding all over the farm's open field.

There was just one difference in all he had seen. In Bobby's place, he drew another boy with small legs that didn't work very well. Behind him, he placed a large board to hold him up straight, with a chest strap so he wouldn't fall off.

The week went by swiftly and it was almost time to go home. Each day, Joe had visited the farm and sketched the chestnut horse even more. His father just smiled, Uncle Albert nodded kindly while Aunty May praised his art. His cousin, Bobby, was the best of the lot. He did his best not to tell Joe what it felt like to ride the horse.

That final afternoon, Dad offered to take Joe one last time to see Ember. It was only polite to say goodbye to the horse since he'd fed her carrots and apples all week long. They all piled into Dad's truck and drove to the farm. Joe was surprised everyone wanted to come along.

Farmer Al stood outside the stables with a grin on his face.

"I'm so glad you got to meet Ember, she'd grown quite fond of you," he said. "But there's one last thing you have to do before you go away."

"What's this?" Joe asked, looking rather confused when Father Al brought Ember out. For on the back of the great, big chestnut horse was a strange looking saddle with a large metal board and a cushion fastened against it. A soft leather strap hung loosely beside it.

"It's a special riding saddle," Farmer Al beamed with pride. "I spent all week making it from your drawings. Your dad told me how well you've sketched all these nights. I thought you might like to see your art in real life."

Joe looked on, completely stunned, because the saddle looked just like he'd drawn.

"Does it really work?" he asked, not wanting to get his hopes up.

"There's only one way to find out," replied Farmer Al. "I'm afraid it won't be fit for a gallop or a canter, but you can certainly sit up high and I'm sure we can manage a trot."

Joe felt tears fill his eyes as he realised Farmer Al had done all this for him. He couldn't find the words to thank the kind farmer, so he squeezed his hand tightly and gave him a hug.

Dad held Joe up and Father Al helped him into the seat, guiding his feet into special stirrups.

"Hold on tight," Farmer Al said with a smile.

Joe had no intention of doing anything else. His whole face lit up as they trotted along.

When it was time to go back home, Dad took a photograph of Joe sitting on Ember, with Farmer Al right beside them. It was a memory Joe would treasure forever.

"I'll keep this safe for the next time you come around," Farmer Al patted the special saddle after Joe got back into his wheelchair. "Never stop dreaming and never stop believing. Just because your life is different doesn't mean you can't achieve your heart's desires."

And those were words Joe never forgot.

STORY 3 – ROYAL BEAUTY

Angie pulled down her woolly hat over her hair and sighed. For a little girl of ten, she had a whole lot of hair. And it wasn't just any type of hair. It was a thick, bushy mess of curls which rose so high up, she stood taller than all the girls in her class.

It never mattered how much she tried to tuck it away, her hair would never sit flat under any hat. She'd tried big ones, and wide ones, flat ones and even small ones. Yet, not a single hat could hold down her unruly mane.

And this was the worst day ever to be stuck with a frizz. Her school had been chosen to meet the Princess Royal, Ophelia, who would be in town to open the new marine museum. Angie would be part of the crowd who stood by the pier and waved and cheered as she came along. There was no way she could stand with them now.

On any other day, her mother would carefully hold Angie's hair down into two neat pigtails with a tub full of gel. Her curly hair would finally lie flat as it dropped all the way past her shoulders in braids. But this morning, her mother was in a rush to get to the hospital where she worked as a doctor. There was no time to braid Angie's hair like she always did.

"But, Mummy, can't I just have it a little bit straightened? I want to look beautiful like all the other girls at school."

"You are beautiful, Angie, with straight hair or not," her mother said. "Besides, it's okay to let your hair out on the pier."

"But all the kids from school will be there!"

"That's perfect. They'll get to see you as I see you every day, my beautiful angel," her mother kissed her head. "Now, hurry or we will both be late."

But Angie knew the girls at school would point and tease her as they giggled. None of them had her big frizzy hair and none of them would understand. So she went back upstairs, snuck into her mother's room, took one of her pretty silk scarves and hid it in her school bag.

Once she got to school, Angie ran to the girls' restroom and tied the big silk scarf across her head. A few stubborn strands still stuck out, but the scarf was so pretty, she was sure it would distract all the others enough.

By the time she got out, everyone was making their way towards the school bus. They were all so excited, no one noticed her scarf or her hair sticking out as they chatted along. Angie sighed with relief and kept her head down until they got to the pier and all piled out.

The crowd moved along and Angie held back until she was the last in the group. She hoped she could see Princess Ophelia all the way from that distance. Her hair might be big, but she wasn't that tall.

As she walked down the pier, a strong sea wind tugged hard at her scarf, but Angie held it down. No one had jeered at her yet, so the scarf had to stay put, at least for another hour or two.

A sleek black car pulled up and the kids all buzzed with delight as the Princess Royal came out. She stood tall and stylish in her lovely green dress. Her hair was in a bun with not a stray strand in sight. She waved a gloved hand and the crowd waved back.

And just as Angie raised her hand to wave with the others, that strong wind came back and tugged once again. This time, with nothing to hold it down, it blew the silk scarf right off Angie's big hair.

With eyes wide as saucers, Angie looked on as the scarf sailed away and towards the Princess Royal. She jumped up as high as she could to catch it, but the wind held on tight and carried it on. It blew the scarf up high at first, as it danced through the air in twirls, and then much lower as it floated over the heads of the kids right next to the princess.

And then, to Angie's pure horror, her mother's silk scarf flew right into the face of the Princess Royal.

Angie gasped, held her chest and burst into tears.

Princess Ophelia plucked the scarf off her face, and then she looked all around the crowd for where it had flown from. All the kids turned to Angie who still cowered at the back. As the princess walked right towards her, Angie wished the ground would open and swallow her up, with her big hair in tow.

But as the princess drew near, Angie was surprised to see she had on a smile.

The princess bent down and held out the scarf.

"I see you've lost this," she said with no anger in her voice, "but it's for the best because you shouldn't hide such lovely hair under a scarf."

Angie looked on in awe. She couldn't believe the Princess Royal was actually talking to her.

"My hair is so big and messy and it looks nothing like the other girls'. I had to keep it covered, it's not fit for meeting a princess at all."

The princess laughed and shook her head, and then she pulled out her shiny phone. She smiled as she showed the screen to Angie with pride in her eyes.

"This is my daughter, Emerald."

On the screen, there was a little girl who looked a lot like the princess, and was just as pretty, except she had thick red hair which was even bigger and curlier than Angie's. In fact, her hair looked like it would need a truckload of gel to hold it all down.

Angie frowned. This had to be a mistake.

"Her hair is…"

She had no words for it.

"Beautiful, isn't it? Just like yours," the princess said.

Angie was still quite confused.

"But she is a princess, she ought to have hair just like yours, all lovely and tamed, and with no stray curls at all."

"Even princesses can have big, messy hair," the princess smiled once more. "It's no fault at all. It has no reflection on what's deep down inside you. So, never hide your true natural beauty. You are both very special, royal princess or not."

And then she tied the scarf around Angie's neck and winked as she left.

Angie was still in shock as all the kids gathered around her, even the ones who would have laughed and pointed at her hair. They could hardly believe all the princess had said. Angie felt herself stand taller as they asked about her hair. She had never felt so proud to have such big, curly hair.

When school time was over and Angie got home, she ran straight to her mother. She had so much to tell her.

"Mummy, Mummy, you'll never believe what happened today!"

"Oh yes, I can believe that, my beautiful angel," her mother said after she had finished her tale. "Your hair has always been beautiful. I'm so glad you finally believe this as well."

And from that day onwards, Angie never hid her hair under a scarf, or any kind of hat; big, wide, flat and even small. Because now she knew that even princesses could have hair just as unruly as hers and still be special. Very special indeed.

STORY 4 – THE FREE GIFT

It was Mother's Day once again and Bradley knew exactly what he was going to get his mother that year with all the pocket money he had saved up. Pink carnations, a box of salted caramel chocolates and a pair of comfy house slippers she had been talking about.

He was even going to make her breakfast in bed, although his father would probably have to deal with the bacon and eggs. Bradley still wasn't great with handling the fiery hob.

Bradley was really pleased with his plans and couldn't wait to see the look on his mother's face when she got all her treats. He was so excited, he barely listened in class all week, and he had to remember not to spill the beans whenever his mother asked why he was so pleased.

But on the Friday before the big Sunday, as Bradley walked home from the bus stop after school, a thought occurred to him.

"Mummy, what happens to Miss Jones on Mother's Day?" Bradley asked his mother with a frown when he got home. "I don't think she has any family, there's never anyone over at hers, so she probably never gets any presents."

Miss Jones was the lady who lived four doors down in a big old white house with a large front garden. In springtime, she sometimes sat on her front porch and waved at Bradley when he walked past on his way from school. She had waved at him that evening, which was what had got him thinking.

Bradley's mother looked surprised, but she answered him. "You're right, I don't think she's got any family. Or, maybe, they live really far away."

Bradley nodded with a determined look on his face. "I'd like to get her something for Mother's Day, but I haven't got any more money." He wished he had some change left over from his shopping spree for his mother.

His mother smiled and looked so proud of him. "You don't need money to show someone that you care about them. You can take her some tulips from our garden. We know she loves flowers, but her garden has none of those. And she would appreciate a visit from you, I'm sure it gets lonely for her sometimes."

And so, on Saturday morning, Bradley picked a dozen bright yellow tulips and tied them up with a red ribbon from Mummy's stash. He combed his hair and put on a smart shirt and pair of trousers. It wasn't quite Mother's Day, but he wanted to save Sunday for his mother. She had called ahead to Miss Jones to find out if it was okay for him to come around for an hour.

It was only ten o'clock when Bradley knocked loud and strong at her front door. He was nervous, but he tried really hard not to show it. Miss Jones opened up with a bright smile and gave him a hug when he handed her the flowers.

"This is very sweet of you, young man. Let's get these in some water so they last a while."

She led the way and Bradley stepped in.

"You'll have to excuse the mess," she said. "I don't have many guests and there's a lot of stuff around."

Bradley's mouth dropped open at what he saw right there in the hallway. All the walls and ceiling were covered with large photos of skies filled with stars. Miss Jones didn't notice his amazement as she walked to the kitchen to fill a vase. Bradley followed closely, still in awe, and saw the kitchen was just the same.

"What's all this for?" he finally asked when Miss Jones had put her flowers away.

"The stars?" she asked, looking around. "I was an astronomer for forty years before I retired, and I still like to look at my stars all day long. Do you know what an astronomer is?"

Bradley nodded eagerly. He loved to sit up at night and watch the stars from his bedroom window. His father even bought him a book that told him what all the clusters in the sky were. He hoped to save up enough for a telescope someday so that he could see all the stars clearly from his room. He knew telescopes cost a lot, which meant it probably wasn't going to happen for a while.

"That's Pegasus," Bradley pointed at one constellation over the kitchen table. He turned and pointed at another just above the doorway and said, "And that's Gemini. Over by the oven is Orion."

"I see you know your stars, young man," Miss Jones said with an impressed voice.

Bradley smiled and pointed out three more.

"If you like these, I think I have a treat for you," Miss Jones said with a wink and led Bradley into her large living room.

This room was even more amazing than the others, completely covered in photos of stars, comets, planets and other bright celestial objects Bradley had never seen before.

But that wasn't what took his breath away. Right by the window stood a large shiny telescope on a three-legged stand.

Bradley squealed with delight and ran to stand beside it. He couldn't believe just how cool it was. Miss Jones was pleased to see how glad he was. She adjusted the eyepiece height so Bradley could look through it. It was even more impressive than he had ever imagined.

"It's much too bright now, but when the sun goes down, I spend many hours gazing up at my stars. Sometimes, I even see the moon in the day."

"One day, I'm going to own a telescope too, so I can watch the stars at night like you do," Bradley declared.

When his hour was up, his mother knocked on the door and Bradley was sad to have to go home. But he thanked Miss Jones politely for sharing her telescope and for teaching him all about the stars on her walls.

The next day, Bradley had just given his mother her presents and served her breakfast in bed when there was a quick knock at the door.

"It's for you, Bradley," his father said, bringing in a long shaped box. "It says on the tag that it's come from Miss Jones."

Bradley was curious as he opened the box. To his surprise, inside was a brand new kid's sized telescope. On a card beside it was a very short note.

"I hope you can make a start with this at night, and then we can compare notes properly next time. From Miss Jones."

Bradley was grateful for the gift, but he couldn't understand why Miss Jones had given him one when it wasn't even his birthday.

"In giving a gift of kindness," his mother explained, "you received something special in return. That's what happens when we do things out of pure love. In life, good follows good."

And so began the beginning of a lifelong friendship. Every Saturday morning, Bradley visited his new friend and learned a little more about the galaxies and the stars. And on the Saturday before every Mother's Day, Miss Jones always got a dozen yellow tulips to put in her vase, right beside her shiny telescope.

STORY 5 – TRUTH BE TOLD

Zotia watched the new kid in class as he shifted from foot to foot at the front of the room. She wasn't the only one staring at him, and it wasn't just because he was new. Or because his hair was so long, it covered his eyes.

The boy was so tall, he was almost Mrs. Nowak's height. And that was incredibly tall for a nine-year-old boy.

"Class, this is Augustyn, or Gus for short," Mrs. Nowak wrote his name down on the board.

Gus looked pretty nervous and played with his hands. Zotia thought she'd be nervous too if she was in his shoes. With everyone gawking, it was hard not to feel odd.

"Why is he so tall?" she heard someone whisper.

"I'm sure he's in the wrong class," someone else said in a low voice.

If Gus could hear this, he didn't say a word. Instead, he started to walk to a desk at the back. And that was when things got even worse. As he walked along, his really long arms started to knock things off people's desks.

A notebook to his right, a ruler to his left. He almost knocked Zotia's pen down as he went. Everyone laughed as he carried along, rather red in the face. Zotia couldn't imagine how awkward he must have felt.

And that wasn't the end of his unfortunate first day. Wherever Gus went, he stuck out like a sore thumb. It didn't really help that he said nothing at all.

"Maybe he's just clumsy," Zotia's best friend, Tesia, said when they met up at break time.

"Maybe he still needs to grow into his body," her mother said when Zotia told her about Gus at home.

"Maybe he's shy," her father replied. "It can't be easy being different and in a new school."

But none of that helped Gus a bit, because he just seemed to stand out more and more. Whenever Zotia tried to talk to him, he turned bright red and walked away. He was too tall for hide and seek, his head poked out from any nook. He might have been good at running fast, but he tripped over each time he tried. When the sports teacher tried basketball, he couldn't even catch the ball.

The only thing Gus seemed any good at was taking care of Spike, the gold coloured bearded dragon who lived in a heated glass tank in class. With so few friends, Gus made sure to feed the little dragon and keep him well. Zotia thought he did a really great job.

One break time, when everyone was out on the playground, Zotia snuck back into the building to get her fidget spinner toy. She'd promised Tesia they could play with it that day. She had snuck in quite often and never been caught. As she crept down the corridor, so she wouldn't get seen, she heard a loud crash come from behind their classroom door.

Afraid she'd get told off, Zotia dashed behind a wall. Then she poked her head out to see who had caused the noise. Just at that moment, someone ran out the door, but they kept their head bent low so Zotia couldn't see who it was. She decided it probably wasn't a good idea to go in to find her spinner toy.

When break time was over and everyone came in, they were shocked to find Spike's glass tank smashed up on the ground. But that wasn't the worst thing at all. The tank was now empty. Spike was nowhere in sight.

Mrs. Nowak was very cross. "We've got to find Spike before he gets hurt. And then we need to find out who knocked down his tank."

Zotia heard the whispers start buzzing around her.

"It had to be Gus."

"It was probably Gus. He's always by the tank with Spike."

"He's so clumsy, he must have knocked it down."

The harsh words kept coming and Gus stood very still. He was clearly too shy to defend himself even then.

But Zotia knew the culprit couldn't have been Gus. She had not seen a face, but the person she saw earlier was nowhere near as tall as him. The problem was, if she spoke up, she would surely get in trouble for sneaking back to class at break time. But if she said nothing, Gus might get all the blame. She had to decide between Gus and herself.

To all of their surprise, Gus suddenly raised his hand. He walked up to Mrs. Nowak with his head held up high.

"I've done a lot of reading on what bearded dragons like. They are very fond of climbing and don't have much fear of heights. If Spike is in here, he'll be up on something high."

And then Gus turned to the back of the classroom. Everyone looked on as he pointed upwards. On top of the supply cupboard at the back of the room, Spike perched near the edge looking calmly around.

And then Zotia realised one important thing. Even with all the mean words spoken about him, Gus had known it was more urgent to find his scaly friend. His bravery gave her the courage to speak loudly as well.

"It wasn't Gus who broke the tank," Zotia raised her hand. "I heard it fall at break time and saw somebody run away before anybody got back. I know it wasn't him because the person who ran out wasn't very tall. In fact, they were just about my height."

She looked around the class and everyone stared back at her, stunned that she had stepped in to help the boy who never spoke. Zotia felt her cheeks go warm as all eyes stayed fixed on her. But then the most amazing thing happened and their stares didn't matter much.

Because, for the first time ever, Gus smiled at her as his eyes lit up with gratitude.

Zotia braced herself for a reprimand. Mrs. Nowak was sure to be very cross. But what she heard next was hard to believe.

"That's very brave of you, Zotia," Mrs. Nowak said. "You knew you could get in trouble for telling the truth, and yet you did so to save Gus. Let this be an example to all you other kids, you should always tell the truth, even when it is hard."

After Mrs. Nowak brought Spike down, she let Gus and Zotia take him to the science lab where they had empty tanks to spare.

"Thanks for standing up for me today," Gus said and put his hand out for a shake.

Zotia took his hand and smiled. "You can show me how to clean Spike's new tank, then we can both take care of him."

And for the second time that day, Gus smiled brightly at her.

STORY 6 – THE LEMONADE STAND

Megan and Lara had a lot of things in common. They both had long brown hair which stopped just past their shoulders. And wide hazel eyes which sparkled when they smiled. They even had the same single dimple on the left side of their faces. But best of all, they were both born on the exact same day, only five minutes apart.

Yes, Megan and Lara were twins and they were identical in every way. They agreed on everything single thing, from the colour of their socks to the pretty bands they wore in their hair.

The girls were playing outside one day when Miss Parker came to visit. She was Mummy's friend who worked with the local arts council, and she always brought cream biscuits.

"We are having a fundraising fair next month," she said, "to raise some cash to fix the leaky theatre roof. All helping hands would be welcomed."

Megan and Lara jumped up and cried, "We'd love to help! We'd love to help!"

"I know what we'll do, let's make some lemonade," Megan suggested.

"That's a great idea! Everyone likes lemonade," Lara agreed.

Mummy also thought it was a great idea and asked Daddy to help them build a stand. He bought some wood and lots of nails and asked the twins to pick the paint.

"Yellow, just like lemonade," they both replied. They didn't have to think at all.

Mummy asked for a list of ingredients to buy when she went to the store.

"Lots and lots of lemons," Megan said.

"And a jar of honey to make it sweet," was Lara's reply.

A day before the fundraising fair, Daddy began to paint the lemonade stand.

"That's much too bright," Megan frowned and shook her head. "That's not the colour of lemonade."

But Lara smiled and nodded at Daddy. "It looks just right, it's nice and bright."

"But it's too bright!"

"No, it's just right!"

The girls kept going back and forth and wouldn't back down even a little bit. They didn't know how to compromise because they had never disagreed before.

"It's okay, girls, I have a plan," Daddy cut in. "I'll paint one half in bright yellow like Lara likes, and the other half we'll tone down like Megan wants."

Daddy painted the top half bright yellow, and wrote the word 'Lemonade' in black. And then he painted the bottom half a faint yellow, and put the cost the girls would charge. They both agreed it looked quite good. And that's how the stand's two shades of yellow came about.

The next morning, Megan and Lara woke up early to make their lemonade. They washed the glass jug, Mummy cut the lemons in half, and they spent all morning squeezing really hard. They mixed the fresh lemon juice with water and honey, and then took sips to test it out.

"It's much too sharp," Lara crinkled her nose. "We'll have to add a lot more honey."

"It's much too sweet," Megan declared, "I think it needs a bit more water."

"I don't want it sharp!"

"I don't want it sweet!"

And once again, they couldn't decide on what to do about their different tastes.

"It's okay, girls, I have a plan," Mummy raised her hands. "Let's split the jug in half and you can both decide what you'd like to add."

So Megan and Lara split the lemonade, and each girl made their own jugs taste just like they liked.

"But I wish Megan would agree with me," Lara crossed her arms with a pout.

"And I wish Lara would side with me," Megan also stuck her bottom lip out.

"It's alright not to agree on everything," Mummy said. "You might look a lot alike, but you're still two different people. When you each have your own opinions, you can put your ideas together and come up with something special."

Megan and Lara thought about it and decided to both take their mixes to the fair.

"This way people can decide which lemonade they'd prefer," they said.

At the fundraising fair, Daddy set up their stand with its two shades of yellow. Mummy helped the girls put out their different jugs and marked one sweet and the other one tart. It was such a hot day, they didn't wait long before a boy came by with his mother.

"I'll like a glass of sweet lemonade, and Mum prefers hers a little sharp."

So, Megan poured a glass of tart lemonade for the mother, and Lara poured a sweet one for the boy.

"This is perfect," the boy said with a sigh.

"And so is mine," his mother replied.

The girls were pleased with their first sale. Very soon, the word got out about their great lemonade. And not just one, but a choice of two. The people queued all the way around the fair and soon the twins ran out of juice.

"We made so much money for the roof!" the girls cheered as Mummy counted their cash.

"I'm so proud of you for volunteering," Mummy said with a big smile, "but I'm even more pleased that you had a problem and found a way to work it out."

STORY 7 — THE DRUM TEACHER

Xavier loved to drum. If he could drum every hour of the day, he certainly would have. His parents made sure he stopped to sleep, brush his teeth, take a bath, eat and drink, and go to school. But he always returned to his drums in the spare room his father had padded out. The noise was much too loud to be let out.

He had a five piece drum kit which he cleaned and checked thoroughly before he played every day. A bass drum, a snare drum, the toms, hi-hats and cymbals. They were his most precious possessions. He had to keep practising so he could get really good and join his favourite band, The Wailing Wiggles.

"Why don't you take some time off to play with Audrey from next door?" his mother had suggested often enough. "Or Lucas who lives just up the road. They seem really nice, and I'm sure you'll have fun."

"If I stop to play with them," Xavier said with a firm shake of his head, "then I won't get any better at playing the drums. And then I'll never become good enough to play with The Wailing Wiggles."

That was all that mattered to him. To be fair, Xavier was very good at mastering his drumming techniques. He was ace at his strokes and pretty cool with his rolls. He was even good at drag ruffs and was learning to paradiddle. He really didn't think his parents understood how difficult all this was. There was certainly no time left to play with the boring kids in the neighbourhood.

One day, as Xavier was riding his bike to school, his mind was filled with thoughts of all he would try on his drums after school. As he rode along with his head in the clouds, he didn't see a huge pothole coming up ahead in the road. He sped right towards it, and before he could stop himself, his bike was thrown over it. And a very confused looking Xavier went flying along with it.

When the doctor examined his X-ray later at the hospital, he frowned and said to Xavier and his parents, "Your arm is broken in two places, you'll need a cast to mend it. It will have to stay on for eight weeks at least."

Eight weeks? But how was Xavier going to practise all the new techniques he was learning? He was just about to start trying out the ratamacue.

"You have to be patient," his father said when Xavier whined about it, "if not, your arm won't heal properly, and that will be much worse for your drumming."

"But what am I going to do for eight weeks?"

"Getting good at something is not always about how often you practise," his mother replied, "it is also important to do some reading about how to master the art."

Xavier wasn't really convinced, but without much of a choice, he decided to give it a try. His parents bought him books on all the great drummers in jazz and rock, and even marching bands. Xavier hadn't realised there was so much more to learn about drummers. With his arm cast in place, he started to read books each day.

"What are you reading?" Audrey, his neighbour, asked when she saw him sitting in the sun with his nose in a big book. It wasn't often she got to see Xavier outside.

"I'm reading about all these amazing drummers who've passed through time," Xavier brushed her off, "I'm trying to get better even though I can't use my hand."

"I've never tried it before, but drumming has always looked like fun," Audrey said. "Will you teach me how to play?"

Xavier looked at her eager face with surprise. He didn't know anyone else who wanted to learn how to drum. They all seemed to think he was silly for trying so hard with something so loud. He'd never considered his neighbour would care one bit about it. With not much else to do, he decided to give it a go.

They used his precious drum kit, which had been standing idly for days. Audrey was a really keen student and quick at picking up the basics. By the end of the afternoon, she had tried both a single and a double stroke roll. Xavier was pleased to see how brightly she smiled when they got to the end of the trial.

His mother was delighted when he came to her room and asked, "Is it okay if Audrey comes around again?" That was a question she'd never thought she'd hear him ask.

"Of course, she can. I am glad you are finally friends."

Not long after that, Audrey and Xavier were sitting in the garden, talking about all the amazing things she had learnt. Lucas, who lived up the road, walked by and overheard their excited chatter.

"You both play the drums?" he asked shyly. "I've got a set of kettledrums. I know it's a bit different, but I'd love to join you when you play."

Xavier was really stunned to hear this. There was another drummer on his street? All this while, his mother had tried to get him to spend time with Audrey and Lucas, and he hadn't given either of them a chance. Now, it turned out they had this one special thing in common.

"I've never played kettledrums," Audrey said excitedly. "Maybe you can teach us how to play those too."

"My dad also has a maraca we can borrow," Lucas offered. "That way, Xavier can play along until his arm gets better."

Xavier was grateful for the thought. He had really missed playing an instrument.

With Xavier so busy hanging out with his new friends and reading all his new books, the dreaded eight weeks whizzed by. Even though he couldn't play his drums with his arm in a cast, he found he was quite satisfied to share them with Audrey and Lucas who came over almost every single day. Except for the days when they went over to Lucas's house to play the kettledrums and the maraca.

And, sometimes, they talked of other fun things, like monster trucks, which Audrey really loved, and super magnets Lucas was really keen on. They even went to watch a marching band who came to town for a parade.

Before he knew it, Xavier was back at the hospital to get his cast taken off. The doctor said he'd healed quite well and his arm was back to good.

"Are you excited to get back to drumming?" his father asked as they left the doctor's room.

Xavier didn't have to think long before he answered. "I missed playing my drums, but I didn't miss them quite as much as I thought. I'll keep practising to get into The Wailing Wiggles, but I'll also make time to hang out with my new best friends."

His parents were pleased to hear this, and they hugged him tightly.

"Always remember that there are others out there who may like all the same things you do. You just have to give them a chance to discover if they do."

STORY 8 – THE SUMMER PARTY

Every year, on Grove Street, there was a birthday party for Valerie Rose. And everyone waited anxiously to see what each one would bring. Because Valerie didn't just throw any regular party, she threw the best birthday parties anyone had ever seen.

One year, there had been a petting zoo with goats, rabbits, llamas and a pony to ride. Another year, three large ball pits had filled her back garden and everyone piled in for a day of fun. And one year, she had three very funny clowns, with one who made giant animals out of balloons for all the kids to take home. There was always a lot to eat and drink, and her cakes almost looked too good to eat.

Valerie's parties were the best, and no one could deny it. But this year, that was all going to end because Valerie was going away. And not just for a little bit of the summer like she sometimes did. Her parents were moving to a new city this time. And, only being nine years old, Valerie was off with them too.

"All those lucky new neighbours Valerie will have soon," Emma sighed.

"What will we have to look forward to?" Kelly asked.

"Nothing else ever happens here in summer," Brandon agreed. "I heard she was planning on having karaoke this year."

The three friends sat on Emma's front porch with sad faces. Valerie would be gone in a week, and it was only the start of the break. There would be nothing to look forward to all summer long.

"But will you miss Valerie?" Emma's mother asked the brooding trio. "Not just her parties and the fun you would have?"

"Of course, we will," Emma piped up. "She's nice to everyone."

"She even invites the kids who don't go to our school," Kelly said.

Emma's mother nodded at this. "Instead of thinking about all the things you'll lose, perhaps you should consider showing her how much you'll miss her. Valerie must be sad to lose all her friends as well."

"I wish there was something we could do to say goodbye to her."

The kids sat back and thought hard for a while.

"Why don't we throw her a farewell party?" Brandon shot up from his chair. "We'll invite all the kids on the street, and we'll make it the best party ever."

The girls perked up at this idea, but Kelly's face suddenly fell.

"Nothing can ever beat Valerie's parties."

"And we haven't got much time, she leaves in a week!"

"It may not be as grand as Valerie's, but we can make it just as fun," Brandon was certain. "If we all work together, I'm sure it will be awesome."

"And maybe, some of the adults can pitch in too," Emma's mother had a smile on this time. "We'll also miss Valerie, she's a sweet and kind little girl."

And so, the three kids put their heads together to come up with a plan

"Keeping it a surprise would be nice, but it also won't be easy," Kelly said.

"We can use the green square at the end of the street," Brandon suggested. "It's surrounded by a brick wall, so she won't see inside."

"I have a great theme in mind," Emma cried. "I think you'll all like it as well."

They all worked really hard, and their parents helped out. By the time the big day arrived, the whole street was buzzing. All the kids had been told it was a surprise, so they had to remember not to say a word to Valerie all week.

At noon on Saturday, Emma, Brandon and Kelly hid with everyone in the walled in square while Valerie's mother brought her there. When they saw her coming, they crouched even lower and tried not to giggle. And when she stepped through the gates, they all jumped out and screamed, "Surprise!"

Valerie squealed with amazement. She had no idea they had been planning anything. And what they had set up was just as astonishing. For all around the square, there were hundreds of bright coloured balloons and party streamers, and a big banner saying, 'We'll Miss You, Valerie!' in large pink letters. And that wasn't all.

The entire square had been transformed. Emma's theme had really been great and an obstacle course had been set up. There were water filled paddling pools with planks placed across them. Semi-circular bands were fixed to the ground for crawling through and jumping over. Water balloons were strung up between trees, waiting to be smashed with big foam bats. There were hopper toys and hula hoops. And all sorts of quirky knickknacks they had thrown together to help finish the course.

Brandon's mother had brought a whole bag of makeup to paint funny faces on kids who wanted to look like tigers or butterflies. Emma's father baked one of his delicious triple chocolate cakes with a thick buttercream frosting, and Kelly's mother had made chilled pink lemonade to go with Emma's father's cake.

Valerie stood staring at everything and everyone. She really couldn't believe her eyes.

"Is this really all for me?"

"We are all going to miss you terribly," Emma said. "We just wanted to let you know."

Valerie had tears in her eyes as she hugged everyone.

"This is the best party I've ever been to. Thank you, everyone."

The three kids' hearts were filled with delight as everyone had a lot of fun that day. Instead of Valerie's goodbye being a sad occasion, they'd managed to make it one filled with love and great memories of laughter. And that was how they learnt that, sometimes, the pure joy of giving is more rewarding than receiving.

DISCLAIMER

This book contains opinions and ideas of the author and is meant to teach the reader informative and helpful knowledge while due care should be taken by the user in the application of the information provided. The instructions and strategies are possibly not right for every reader and there is no guarantee that they work for everyone. Using this book and implementing the information/recipes therein contained is explicitly your own responsibility and risk. This work with all its contents, does not guarantee correctness, completion, quality or correctness of the provided information. Misinformation or misprints cannot be completely eliminated.

Printed in Great Britain
by Amazon

59110347R00026